David Roberts Dungan

Prohibition VS. License

David Roberts Dungan

Prohibition VS. License

ISBN/EAN: 9783742899873

Manufactured in Europe, USA, Canada, Australia, Japa

Cover: Foto ©Andreas Hilbeck / pixelio.de

Manufactured and distributed by brebook publishing software
(www.brebook.com)

David Roberts Dungan

Prohibition VS. License

vs

LICENSE.

BY

D. R. DUNGAN,

Author of "On the Rock.

" License to make the strong man weak ?
License the wife's fond heart to break ?
License to kindle hate and strife ?
License to whet the murderer's knife ? "

OSKALOOSA, IOWA:
CENTRAL BOOK CONCERN,
1875

PREFACE.

'The serial published some months ago in the *Evangelist*, entitled " Prohibition *vs* License," awoke much interest in the subjects discussed, and there have been so many demands for back papers, which cannot be supplied, we have, after many urgent requests by prominent citizens, both in and out of the church, consented to publish these articles in tract form.

Consequently we have re-arranged the articles for the form in which they are now presented. Besides we have added one chapter to the original matter.

As to the contents of the work, you must be your own judge. But I sincerely hope that it may contribute something toward that sentiment that will enable us to deal justly and sensibly with the evils of intemperance.

PROHIBITION vs LICENSE.

CHAPTER I.

A STATEMENT OF THE QUESTION, WITH INTRO-
DUCTORY REMARKS.

For many years temperance men have been
struggling to put away the iniquity of drunkenness, and reclaim the fallen. Much has been
done, but very much yet remains to be done.
That intemperance is an evil, every reader of
these pages is supposed to fully believe. You
are supposed also to know that the sale and use
of intoxicating liquors as a beverage, is the greatest of financial curses. And also that the use that
is now made of these liquors, stands in the way of
the education of our people, withholding many
hundreds of thousands of our children from
our public schools, and in the way of our religion, and all good morals. Such primary les-
sons you are supposed to have learned. But
the practical question of to-day is, how shall
we free our country from the traffic in intoxicants? Here we may differ. We do not claim
that our judgment is at all infallible in such
matters, yet we have had enough experience in
the war with the giant to entitle our thoughts
to some consideration.

The first view of the subject to which we pay our respects is, that we must license the traffic thus putting it under the control of law. In order to such a license a man may be required to have so many free-holders in the precinct, to ask for such license for said saloonist, assuring the proper officers that he is a gentleman of good moral character and standing. Thus will we be able to prevent the lowest class of men, from obtaining license or engaging in the business. That any man supposes that there is any common sense in that plea, taxes our credulity greatly to believe. In the first place, no man of good moral character would ever want to sell whiskey. And in the second place, any free-holder that would go on a man's bond in order that he might have license to poison his fellow-men, would not be particular whether the man had a character or not; in the opinion of such men, character is not essential to the business! Besides, it is superlative folly to talk of controlling a crime by licensing it. We are not so simple about other things. No man pleads for a license to steal or murder, and yet these crimes are far less injurious to the public than that of selling whiskey. It comes then, so far as we may reason the question, to this: to sell intoxicants is a crime, and cannot, therefore, in the very nature of things be licensed, but must be prohibited.

CHAPTER II.

It is assumed that intoxicating beverages will be sold and drank; and that while the evil cannot be prevented, it may be so regulated as to make it less injurious to the world by preventing that kind of houses in which men are most likely to be ruined.

But if licensing the liquor traffic resulted as they argue that it should, still the system would be wrong. If it would prevent the lowest kind of doggeries and only permit those approximating more nearly to respectability, the result would be all the worse. No man becomes a drunkard, at most but few, from the temptations held out at the lower order of saloons. The young man does not see there the kind of dram-drinker that he would prefer to be; their noses are too blue and their clothes too tattered and torn; and his self-respect absolutely shrinks from going in with such a filthy set. But it is when he passes one of those brilliantly illuminated halls, where no drunkards are permitted to obtain anything to drink; where Judge —— goes, and where honorable men "not a few" obtain "a little wine for the stomach's sake and their often infirmities;" where everything is done up in the most gen-

teel style that business of such a nature will
permit, that he feels disposed to pass an hour in
watching a game of billiards, and even to take
a glass of some *"perfectly harmless temperance
drink."* Now what endangers public safety in
the matter of intemperance, is the constantly
recruiting efforts that are being made. If there
were not six hundred thousand new tipplers
added to the roll annually, drunkards would
become extinct in a few years. Sixty thousand
of them go to an untimely grave every year,
which would soon thin their ranks if it were
not for the fact that their places are being filled
by others who are decoyed into the meshes of
iniquity by the more attractive places and the
more honorable gentlemen who go there. But
if the saloons were all kept on the low order
that some of them are, but very few would be
deceived by them. But when the business can
be elevated to the plane proposed by the license
system, then there is danger; for deception is
then made easy.

Right here, again, I fault the system, in that
it refuses liquor to the man that is in the habit
of becoming intoxicated, or who is in a state
of intoxication, as well as to minors. True,
none of these restrictions are regarded by rumsellers; for a man that is mean enough to
engage in that business has no real respect for
the law. And the idea that he could ever find

a man too drunk or unsteady, or too young to
need a drink if he has the money to pay for it,
is preposterous in the extreme. What does he
know or care about such things? What he
does business for is the money. If he gets it,
he is satisfied. How he gets it, he has decided
to be none of your business.

But suppose that they had a conscience like
other men, and would follow out the demands
of law. What then? Only this : they would
sell by the dram to a young man until his system would become so entirely under the influence of the poison, and his common sense
should so fail, and he would lose his self-respect
to the extent of becoming willing to be known
as a drunkard, then they would shut him out
of doors and declare him an unfit subject to
deal with. But when a man has fallen so low
as that, he will send for it by the quantity and
drink it somewhere else. While this pretended
decency of the law would not protect the people that it had permitted first to be ruined, it
would only become the more powerful to en-
tangle the young and unsuspecting into that
web of iniquity from which they find themselves unable to escape.

But some one says, it is a source of revenue,
and asissts in educating our children. I think
if our children are to be educated on this kind
of tax, it will be a feature of syntax (sintax)

not before understood. Let us look this thing
in the face. One hundred producers make absolute net gain of one thousand apiece. Out
of this all their expenses are to be met. Would
it increase their ability to educate their children
to take half of their produce and burn it?
And yet they would better burn it than rot it
and make it into alcohol to poison themselves
with! Now what is not proper for a hundred
men to do, is not proper for a thousand, or a
million, or a nation to do. The truth is, in so far
as the license system permits the sale of intoxicants, it withholds both the ability and the
disposition to educate the children. What is
gained, therefore, by license in the way of ed-
ucational funds has been lost a thousand times
in morals, industry, stability, intelligence, and
general prosperity. My whole nature spurns
the idea of gathering a little tax at the expense
of blood! Gathered from the dying groans of
the drunkard, the sighs of the broken-hearted
widow, and the piercing cries of helpless, hun-
gry, orphans! Let us cease to lull our con-
sciences to sleep by such feeble attempts at
logic as that of taxing whiskey to educate our
children.

We have been trying to show that the license
system is wrong in its very nature. That is,
we have furnished a few specimens of practical
injustice. To those who have devoted much

time to the subject, we have already said more than was strictly necessary. But it is not every good temperance man that is fully informed on all these questions. Hence the necessity of having a fair understanding with our friends. I cannot leave this part of my subject without further reference to the essential error of the license system.

If the sale of intoxicating drinks is a proper and profitable pursuit, then why fine it beforehand? The license system reminds me of the man who always kicked his boys whenever they passed him. He said if they did not need it then, they soon would. So our law seems to regard the traffic in liquors as being essentially wrong, and therefore to be punished by fine to begin with.

I hate a monopoly in anything, for it can only lead to tyranny; at least such is its history. But why a monopoly should be allowed in rum-selling more than in anything else, I do not know. As to its preventing bad men from selling, is the merest nonsense in existence.— Scarcely will any other man seek for or obtain a license; for no man who has the cause of humanity at heart will, understandingly, engage in such a nefarious business. Hence it makes money the standard of character necessary to engage in this traffic. Now, I think that any poor wretch who may want to deal out poison by the ten cents' worth, ought to have the same right to take the life of his fellow man for money that the rich man has. As this is a free country, let him exercise his gift. The whiskey that he would sell would only make loafers, loungers, vagabonds; brutalize, debauch, ruin, blunt all the finer sensibilities of the soul, cause poverty, destroy the peace in the family and in society, dethrone the reason and wreck the manhood; sow the seeds of degradation and death; bloat and blacken and blister and blight the body; fill the country with helpless orphans and broken-hearted widows, and cover the land with shame and disgrace, just the same as that which is sold by that more fortunate gentleman who is able to sport "a good moral character!" And hence the injustice of our law must be apparent, as it refuses one of the inalienable (?) rights to a poor, worthless creature, for no other reason than his want of money to buy license to kill men and be happy and respectable!

But there is sometimes a plea made for the license law like this: We must license the sale of rum, so that it may come legitimately under the control and regulation of law.— Such a plea, however, is so utterly void of any common sense that we would here pay it no attention, but for our respect for those who offer it. There are many crimes of minor importance that our law deals with by prohibiting them. If any man would argue that we must license theft, or larceny, or fraud, in order to bring it under the control of law, it would only excite contempt for the author. The argument itself is really based upon the idea that selling whiskey is not wrong in itself; but it is only when abused by being conducted in an improper manner. This, however, we have already considered, and have decided that the traffic in intoxicants is the most withering, blighting curse that has ever befallen our country. Still further we have seen that when the saloon is raised in the scale of its degradation looking toward decency, its power for evil is increased; that it then becomes capable of deceiving many who would never be decoyed into one of those lower haunts of vice. Hence, the saloon business is a crime against humanity, and, like any other crime, cannot be regulated. That is not what law proposes to do with crime. Suppose that we talk sentimentally about regulating murder by law? Our logic would then only equal that of those who argue that we must regulate the rum traffic—by a license law!

If a man must buy a license in order to sell whiskey, I can see no reason why he ought not to be permitted to drink it in the same way. When a man drinks he endangers not only himself but his property, and the lives of other men, and even the lives of his wife and children. A man is therefore criminal when he does that which he knows leads to destruction and misery, or, at least, to the probability of such things. Now if crime is to be regulated by law, especially that of the sale of alcohol, I cannot see why a man should not be required to take out a license to drink it. This, too, might go to increase the school fund! And a man would then have purchased the right to any kind of a debauch that might happen to suit his peculiar taste. It would then be his right to squander his means with the "gentlemen of good moral character and standing" who have been employed by the people to corrupt their sons, impoverish the community, and ruin the country. Having purchased this liberty with a great sum of money, he would then be free, not only to drink whiskey, but to commit whatever crimes it might prompt. And whatever of infamy, of theft, of lust unbridled, of brutality, beastiality and loathsomeness that would naturally follow his inebriety, would have all been arranged and provided for by the prepaid indulgence! No man could then call in question his right to beat his wife for not having dinner ready for her lord, when there was nothing to make it of, or no fuel to cook it with, for this would be one of the consequential privileges that he would have purchased in obtaining his license! This

would surely make it all right. No one could
object to a gentleman like that having the privilege of wrecking his manhood, impoverishing
his family, and losing his own soul, especially
if he would first pay a small sum of money into our school fund for such a pleasure and privilege! Besides, it would not at all inconven-
ience him. He could as easily prove a good
character before the law as the saloon-keeper.
Let the license law then be made consistent
with itself, or let it be repealed.

CHAPTER III.

WHAT IS DONE IN THE SALOONS AND WHAT SALOON-KEEPERS KNOW OF THEIR TRAFFIC.

The saloon-keeper knows that his business is
infamous ; that he is hurrying men into the
grave ; that he is impoverishing the people ;
that he is corrupting society. Rev. John Russell of Detroit, Michigan, tells us that in a lecture one night on the subject of temperance he
spoke in the presence of a leading rumseller.
That evening he happened to be unusually severe on saloon-keepers, throwing at them what

his insight would enable him to say of their death-dealing trade. After the lecture he was introduced to the liquor man, when the following conversation was had:—

Saloonist.—"Well, Mr. Russell, you were a little hard on whiskey-sellers."

"Yes, sir, I did the best I knew, yet I was not vain enough to suppose that I was capable of equalling the facts."

"I see, sir,"said the saloonist "that you do not understand the infernal business as well as I do."

There is many a truth told in a jest, and I think that that was one. Those men know more of their own meanness than we do. They are not at all ignorant of the results of their business. They are by no means proud of their work. The machinist, the farmer, the tailor, the boot-maker, are all proud of their most successful efforts. But if the saloon-keeper sees one of his customers wallowing in a drunken fit, he does not invite the attention of the passing crowd to the evidences of his success in his "legitimate calling." No, indeed, he feels that the less said about his success the better.

"Why don't these "*gentlemen of good moral character*" attend the State fairs and compete for the prize? Why do the committees constantly forget to advertise the regular prizes for the most successful effort in this "honorable

calling?" I imagine one of them renting a
stall on the fair-ground, and putting into it a
sample of his work. And when the proper
committee passes that way, he calls their attention to his work.—"Now, gentlemen, do you see
that poor, thinly clad, half-starved, pale, deject-
ed looking woman there in that corner?"
"Yes."
"Well, those ragged, starved, frightened
looking children are hers; arn't they woe-be-
gone, though?"
"They are indeed."
"Now, gentlemen, look at that bloated, stu-
pid, idiotic, ragged, don't-care-a-continental
looking specimen of the genus homo? Isn't he
about as low down as you can get 'em on top
of dirt? eh? Did you ever see a more com-
pletely demoralized, befuddled, dumbfounded,
everlastingly-done-for piece of humanity, since
Judas Iscariot slew Job with a cane? Now
did ye? eh?"
"Never."
"That under lip didn't always swing the
way it does now. He was drinking one day
and got into a row with Ike Plunket and some
how in the affray he got his lip split, his jaw
bone cracked, and three of his under teeth
knocked out. That left eye was knocked out
in another fuss; and at another time he fell out
of a carriage and his head struck a rock and

made that peeled place you see there. All that has been done by the whiskey that was gotten at my poison shop. You see, gentlemen, that he was a downright good looking man once."

"Now, gentlemen, this man and his family have been reduced to this wretched condition in three years' time. It was one of the happiest families I ever saw. They had a nice, cozy little home, all their own ; he wrought at carpentry and came home at six every evening ; always found his smiling, happy wife waiting for him at the little gate. Their rooms were the quintessence of taste and refinement. They loved each other with a purity and perfectness that would do credit to angels. Their prayers and songs went up higher, and passed the stars with greater ease and swifter velocity than those sent up from any church in the land, for they emanated from as pure hearts as the earth could boast. He was a gentleman of credit and respectability, and she was one of the cheeriest, happiest, little Christian women that ever lived. Really, sirs, when we took this man in hand, protected as he was by his love of home, sustained by his self-respect and fortified by his religion, I looked upon him as one of the most doubtful and difficult cases I ever saw. But I had a respectable saloon. Honorable men took light drinks in my house, and through their influence, and our professions of personal

friendship, we decoyed him, little by little, until
he would spend time with us to the neglect of
business. After that, of course, it was easy.
And now, at the end of three years, he is before
you, the miserable apology for a man that you
see him. He is now but the merest shadow of
his former self. But, sirs, he is not the only
evidence of our skill and accomplishment in
the trade. Gradually has the beauty faded
from the cheek of that woman; her eyes have
lost their lustre; tears, instead of smiles indi-
cate the changed condition of her heart. Shame
and disgrace and poverty are her portion; her
home has been sold; joy has faded from her
heart; and now as I have turned her husband
over to the lower order of slaughter-pens, I
think that six months more will end his life and
hers too, and send the little boys to the poor-
house. Can't you give me the blue ribbon?"

A few men may be found in the liquor business who may not know the evil that must nec-
essarily result from their work. Such men
may be persuaded to desist from the death-dealing traffic. Such men only need to have the
facts clearly stated, and their better natures
would revolt at their occupation. But the
great majority of them are not ignorant of what
they are doing. And about the only way to
cause them to repent, is to prohibit them from
their chosen work, or so instruct and persuade

the public that they will cease to have custom.
And yet I think it possible for an old, hardened,
conscience-seared saloon-keeper to be regener-
ated. Six years in the penitentiary, four years
in the house of correction, and three or four
years in some good water-cure establishment
might elevate him to the moral plane of ordinary thieves, when his entire conversion might
be anticipated without any unnecessary delay.
I humbly beseech those who have not yet lost
all interest in a future state of being to repent
while they can. There is an old stanza that
says,

> " As long as the lamp holds out to burn,
>   The vilest sinner may return."

But I am not sure that the sentiment is correct. I believe it possible for a man to sin
away all his moral powers, thus forcing himself
beyond recovery. Not that divine mercy
would not pardon if he came, but he may ren-
der himself unable to come. A man may have
forgiveness for having sinned against God, but
when he sins against himself, he may have gone
beyond the reach of mercy, for he may be unable to provide pardon and the required release.
It may be thought that we are a little too
severe on those engaged in the sale of rum.
But I do not think that I have in any way ex-
aggerated the evils of the rum traffic. " What
I have written, I have written." If I should

ever try to call a man by all evil names and
accuse him of being guilty of all crimes, I
would feel satisfied by just calling him a rum-
seller.

If my son should be met by a highwayman
and robbed of his hard-earned fortune I would
encourage him to go out again into the world
and earn another. His health and strength
would be left, his credit would yet be good,
and the world would yet be before him. True,
I should not feel well toward the villain who
did the deed, but to estimate the crime proper-
ly, I am compelled to say, that he has only
taken my son's fortune, all else are his. But if
he is met the second time, and not only robbed
of his fortune, but also of his life, and is
brought to me but a mangled corpse, I would
weep only as a father could weep. This would
be an end of earthly hopes, and the murderer
would be infinitely worse, in my estimation,
than the highway robber who took only the
money but left his person and his life untouch-
ed. But if some bloodless villian should decoy
him into a saloon and cause him to become a
drunkard and thus lose, not only his money,
but his health, his honor, his integrity, his
common sense, his love of truth, his life, and
even his soul, I would regard him as being in-
comparably meaner than either of the first two.
Even the murderer stops with taking the life

and money of his victim, but the rum-seller takes all that life holds dear; disgraces even the relatives of the unfortunate man; prepares him for the abode of the damned and then sends him to that Gehenna "where the worm dieth not and the fire is not quenched." Such men are not simply dealing out death to a worthless class of humanity; they have first made them worthless; for some of the brightest intellects of the nation have been ruined by this tempter. Appetite, when poisoned, has proved more than a match for their minds and they have fallen a prey to the vice. But for the rum trade they would have been honorable men in society, skilled in the practice of medicine, and ornaments and potencies for good in our legislative halls. But they have been ensnared by the temptation, have fallen by its power, and are made to fill drunkard's graves.

But I will yet pray that God may pity the saloon-keeper, the legislators who will pass a license law, and the men who vote for them.

CHAPTER IV.

THE KIND OF LIQUORS THAT ARE DEALT OUT
AT THE PRESENT TIME BY SALOONISTS AND
DRUGGISTS, AND EVEN SOLD AT WHOLE-
SALE.

I have been requested to speak a word on the
subject of poisoning liquors. I fear that many
do not realize that they cannot get any pure
liquors. We once saw old men stagger on the
streets. Now, if given to intoxication, they
do not live to be old. A few years' use of the
stuff that is now sold for whiskey, will put any
ordinary man on the cooling board. The
physician who will now prescribe brandy as a
medicine, and leave the patient to be supplied
from the market, must either be a consecrated
dunce or have an interest in a coffin shop. A
few. *"fanatics on temperance,"* less than a year
ago, in Lincoln, Nebraska, obtained twelve
samples of liquors in that city and submitted
them to Prof. Aughey, of the State University,
for an analysis. Here is his report :

LINCOLN, NEB., April 25, 1874.

REPORT TO THE LINCOLN CITY TEMPERANCE SOCIETY.

In accordance with your request, I have made a careful analysis of
the liquors brought me two weeks ago. The following is the result:

No. 1. " Detwiler's Black Mariah."

1. Sugar of lead, 8 grains to the quart. 2, Strychnine, a large

amount. 3, Strontia. 4, Benzine. 5, Potash. 6, Brazil wood. 7, Alcohol, 17 per cent.

No. 2. *"Quick's best whiskey."*

1. Sugar of lead, 8 grains to the quart. 2, Strychnine. 3, Strontia. 4, Potash. 5, Benzine. 6, Brazil wood. 7, Alcohol, 18 per cent.

No. 3. *"Klutch's whiskey."*

1. Sugar of lead 8½ grains to the quart. 2, Strychnine. 3, Strontia. 4, Potash. 5, Logwood. (*No Alcohol.* Please Note.)

No. 4. *"Hodskin's whiskey."*

1. Sugar of lead, 8½ grains to the quart. 2, Strychnine 3, Strontia. 4, Potash. 5, Logwood. [*No Alcohol.* Please note.]

No. 5. *"Leighton and Brown's best port wine."*

1. Sugar of lead, 8 grains to the quart. 2, Potash and soda carbonates. 3, Logwood. 4, Alcohol, 9 per cent.

No. 6. *"Baily and Andrew's whiskey·"*

1. Sugar of lead, 7 grains to the quart. 2, Strychnine. 3, Potash. 4, Strontia. 5, Benzine. 6, Brazil wood. 7, Alcohol, 15 per cent.

No 7. *"Brock and Co's. port wine."*

1. Sugar of lead. 2, Potash, and Soda carbonates in large quantities. 3, Logwood. 4, Alcohol, 9 per cent.

No. 8. *"Kellogg and Reed's brandy."*

1. Sugar of lead, 7 grains to the quart. 2, Strontia. 3, Brazilwood. 4, Alcohol, 25 per cent.

No. 9. *"McYaughlin's gin."*

1. Sugar of lead, 5 grains to the quart. 2, Strychnine. 3, Strontia. 4, Potash. 5, Benzine. 6, Alcohol, 16 per cent.

No. 10. *"Zerung and Harley's angelica wine."*

1. Sugar of lead, 2 grains to the quart. 2, Potash, and soda carbonates. 3, Brazil wood. 4, Alcohol, 12 per cent.

No. 11. *"Zerung and Harley's best Bourbon whiskey."*

1. Sugar of lead, 6 grains to the quart. 2, Strontia. 3, Brazilwood. 4, Alcohol, 12 per cent.

No. 12. "S. S. Brock's common whiskey."

1 Sugar of lead 9 grains to the quart. 2, Strychnine. 3, Strontia. 4, Potash. 5, Benzine. 6. Brazil-wool. 7, Alcohol 15 per cent

This analysis is not exhaustive, as I did not separate the sugar which some of the liquors contained in the form of caramel, or the cayenne pepper which all the whiskies contained, more or less. The poisonous substances, however. I carefully separated. The absolute amount of sugar of lead, strychnine and strontia, was remarkably large. The poisonous qualities of these substances are so well known, that nothing here needs to be said about them.

In many of these liquors there is strychnine enough in a quart, to kill a man if it were taken separate from any other mixture and at one dose ; the same is true of the sugar of lead.

In good whiskey, the amount of alcohol should be from 40 to 50 per cent. But in these liquors, it ranged only from 15 to 25 per cent ; the larger percentages belonging to the brandies and gin.

As good liquors as some of these whiskies, could be profitably manufactured for thirty cents a gallon ; and *none* of these liquors are what they purport to be.

If any one doubts that these poisons are found in common liquors, if such doubter will come to the University laboratory in the afternoon I will separate and precipitate lead, strontia, &c., in his presence.

Respectfully submitted,

SAM'L AUGHEY,

Prof. of Chemistry in University of Nebraska.

When this report was published, there was " no small stir " in the city. Some saloon-keepers declared that they did not know that they had been dealing out such poisons. But the wholesale dealers, and some of the druggists were involved ; some of the most interested, denied the correctness of the analysis, but they did not dare to put it to the proof. Many of those who had been drinking these liquors, quit their use and took to beer as a substitute,

not knowing that beer is as badly dealt with as
anything else. At best, it is but a miserable
slop, containing but about two per cent of nu-
tritious aliment, the rest being hop tea, alcohol,
and rotten swill.

I have noted these things that you may
realize what we authorize, when we license the
sale of these things. For what is done in Lincoln, is done elsewhere. I do not pretend that
the honesty of whiskey sellers in that city is
equal to the sugar of lead in their liquors, and
yet I suppose that they will compare favorably
with rumsellers in general. There may be
men among them that do not know that they
are dealing in such poisons, but such men will
discontinue the business when they come to
know what they are dealing in, if they have
a single spark of honesty or humanity left.

If our bakers were known to sell poisoned
bread, we could prosecute them for it. But
when men sell the most loathsome poisons in
liquors, we must permit it! Does any one say
that we only license the sale of pure liquors?
I call his attention to the fact that the license
law provides no means for preventing the sale
of any kind of stuff that may suit the saloonist
best.

CHAPTER V.

WHAT WE HAVE GAINED.

We have no* particular desire just now to deal with the use of alcohol as a medicine. Yet we freely give our opinion that it contains neither food nor medicine. But if it may be beneficial in the healing art, then it is not a food, even though it were not poisoned. Hence as a beverage it should be prohibited. No man will be guilty of such folly in the use of arsenic, strychnine, or any other powerful drug. He would not presume to know his own condition —never having studied medicine, and prescribe so much calomel. But the manner in which this whole matter is treated in our license law keeps up the idea that it is only the abuse of the thing as a beverage that makes it an evil. While the truth is it is neither good for a sick man nor a well man, and is never taken into the human system except for injury. My opinion is that when we come to be freed from the delusion that has so long obscured the sight of the people of America and Europe that we will demand of our men of medicine to discontinue its use.

I apprehend that the time is coming when those who will provide anything that can intoxicate as an entertainment will be regarded not only with suspicion but they will be looked upon as those whose education has been sadly neglected.

We are sometimes given to despondency. But when we think of the lethargy and thoughtless indifference on this subject a few years ago, and compare the public sentiment of those times with the activity and energy manifested in the matter to-day, we have reason to thank God and take courage. And yet we do not expect that time alone will remove the evil. We are fully convinced that while we are gaining ground, that we must continue to fight until the last saloon is closed and the last distillery ceases its operations.

Public sentiment has already decided, and all men know that the sale of alcohol is an abominable business. Once our taverns had a bar, they all had them ; indeed, tavern and whiskey were nearly synonymous terms. Every public gathering had to be disgraced with rum. A man could not harvest without whiskey. It was thought to be indispensible, in wet weather, to keep a man dry ; in dry weather to prevent him from being too dry ; in hot weather to cool him, and in cool weather to warm him ! For wounds, bruises, and snake-bites, it was the only panacea. But the world advances. Alcohol has been convicted of all the crimes known to history. It has been dismissed ,from the harvest and the public gathering; in the respectable hotel it has no longer a place. It has been crowded out of the public walks and elbowed out of decent society. If it exists in connection with the hotel, it is put off down in the cellar, or out of the hearing of respectable guests. If a man opens a saloon on the street, he put's a screen in the door for the simple reason that it has become so disrespectable to attend such places that young men would not go there unless there was something to protect them from the public gaze.

On the other hand, temperance is becoming popular. Almost all men now claim to be temperance men. If the saloon-keepers of the nation were to come together in council, the first resolution that they would likely pass would be that they are in favor of temperance. They would only claim that they differed from other men in the manner of promoting the good cause. Of course all this would be buncombe, but it shows which way the wind blows.

CHAPTER VI.

THE LICENSE SYSTEM IS WRONG IN ITS VERY NATURE, AND UNSUCCESSFUL IN PRACTICE.

The principle of the liquor license is radically wrong in that it prohibits the smaller crimes and licenses and permits the greater ones. You do not need me to tell you over again the expenses and financial burden that this traffic lays on the shoulders of the honest yeomanry of the country. It is not necessary for me to say that its wholesale cost in 1873 was one billion and four hundred and eighty-seven million dollars; that it employed the time of six hundred thousand bar-tenders; that it incurred the expenses of the room rent of one hundred and sixty thousand buildings; that it monopolized the time of two million men, made vagrants by drink; that it cost the country ninety million dollars to try the cases in court occasioned by drunkenness; that it sent sixty thousand to a drunkard's grave and a drunkard's hell; these are only some of the smaller evils. If our railroads cost on an average twenty thousand dollars per mile, the seventy-two thousand miles in the United States have cost one billion four hundred and forty thousand dollars,—lacking more than forty thousand, of equalling the wholesale cost of alcohol for a single year.

Slavery had its evils; it enslaved four millions of human beings for whom Christ died. But alcohol enslaves the souls and bodies of a much greater number. African slavery may have been a financial curse to the nation, but its financial evils would not equal a mill on a thousand dollars of the cost of rum. Our civil war cost us much, in money, in life, in anxiety, and in corruption, but nothing to compare with the cost of alcohol in these respects. We would better sport an internal war with all its train of evil results, than continue the sale of rum.

Now if our government would license six hundred thousand sleight-of-hand performers, to go about over the country and dement as many young men as could be persuaded into their deceptive arrangements, we might be content for, though our sons would be unsafe, their lives would be left and we would hope to find some treatment that would restore them. If we should give permits to steal and plunder, still we might protect ourselves against these legal thieves, and our lives and health and mental strength and honor would be left. Should four hundred thousand murderers obtain privilege to engage in their business by assuring the government that they are "*gentlemen of good moral character*," it might be inconvenient and unsafe, but still we leave behind us a good name and

character that might be copied by our children,
and take with us a clean soul out into the presence of God. But the rum trade is the full
equal of all these crimes; it ruins the health,
corrupts the morals, blunts the finer sensibilities
of the human heart, bloats and poisons and
brutalizes the man until he becomes a demon
incarnate; robs him of his hard earning, wrecks
his manhood and dements his brain; it takes
away his respectability and clothes him in rags;
it takes the bread from the wives and children
of its dupes, and leaves them broken-hearted, if
not broken-headed, as well as disgraced and
penniless; it corrupts and blights the soul and
sends the man to an untimely grave. Now I
plead in the name of justice and common sense,
that our law should not be guilty of the incon-
sistency of prohibiting those smaller crimes and
licensing one that lifts its hydra-headed uncov-
ered ugliness in fearful altitude above all others
of this age. Yes sir, if crime must be licensed
and made respectable, then license men to train
rattle-snakes, that they may fasten their poisonous fangs into the very hearts of innocent children; license them to keep mad-dogs for the
destruction of life and happiness; license them
to engage in these comparatively harmless
things, but let us listen to the sighs and groans
coming up from the graves of the drunken
dead, and hear the ceaseless heart-piercing wails

of their ruined families, before we license the rum traffic.

If only our people could be made to realize their responsibility, that what we do by the hands of another we do as really as if we acted independently of such an agent, that when we make a law that permits crime to run riot at noonday, and that when men are killed as the result of such a law, that we are guilty of the blood of a brother, we might be still more aroused on the question than what we are. Having witnessed the utter incompetency of the license system to bring us any relief from the evils of intemperance, finding that it has failed, as it must, of any practical good to those States that have tried it, seeing that it is wrong in the nature of things, to license that which is evil, and that the sale of whiskey is the greatest evil of the present time, we ask, are we not ready now to deal sensibly with this question? While men are ready to exercise common sense in reference to all other crimes, we wonder how long it will be before the crime of rum-selling may be dealt with in justice? In another chapter we will tell you why we make haste so slowly in this work of redeeming our country from the " gall of bitterness and bond of iniquity." But from all that is now before us, we arrive at the inevitable conclusion that it is the duty of our law-makers to prohibit, not only the crime of drunkenness, but the still worse crime of making drunkards.

CHAPTER VII.

A MAN HAS THE RIGHT TO DO WITH HIS OWN AS HE PLEASES, ONLY WHEN HE DOES NOT INJURE OTHERS THEREBY.

It sometimes argued that a man has a right to do with his own as he pleases, and therefore men and laws have no right to interfere with his business. If he chooses to sell whiskey then it is his right to do so, since it is his property. But if that argument is good then the license system is wrong, since it may debar some from this inalienable right, they not being able to pay the requisite amount.

But it is not true in the absolute, that a man may do as he pleases with his own. Since such a privilege granted to the unprincipled would work the insecurity of the person or property of another. By a wrong or vicious use of his own, a man might do violence to other men, which he has no natural, and should have no legal right to do. Hence, a man may not burn down his own house, since, if he does not endanger the houses of other men, or destroy the life of some one within, yet he destroys the

property of the common wealth, and by so
much, injures the community as he burns up
its capital. A man may not ignite a prairie
fire when by so doing he renders the property
of another unsafe. The land might be his own
but it makes no difference in the eyes of law
and justice. If a man should start a glue man-
ufactory in the heart of our city, though his
work would be a profitable one in many respects, yet its fumes would create an unhealthy
and offensive atmosphere. It would be dispens-
ed with, and no claims of a right to do as he
pleases with his own, would protect him in the
eyes of a refined and sensible community. To
keep a hotel is right, to keep hogs is well
enough, to give them the offal of the house is
judicious and economical, but where swine and
slops become offensive to the health and happiness of the people, neither the city fathers nor
the citizens listen to any claims of individual
rights, but demand that *the nuisance shall be
abated*. A man might buy lots in this city and
proceed to construct a powder magazine thereon,
under the pretense of a right to do as he pleases
with his own. But the people would be indig-
nant at the idea. Nor would he be permitted
to continue in his business. This plea then
must be so circumscribed, that when a man
does as he pleases with his own he will not
please to do that which will injure other per-

sons, or even endanger their lives or their property.

The more common or popular plea, however, that is now made by rumsellers and their political abettors is, that it is the inalienable right of every man to eat and drink that which he pleases. If this can be established their work is light. Their right to sell that which it is right for men to use could hardly be called in question.

But let us examine this assumption a little. Man has some things in common with the animal creation, such as flesh, blood, bones, instinct, and intuition. He has also other mental qualities not possessed by animals in general. Those declare that he is an animal while these affirm his superiority over all other earthly existences. When man gratifies his appetite or his lust, he yields to the demands of his inferior nature. The instinct of animals is their guard against the violation of law. But man has been left without such protection, for his superior powers of thought and reason must be his guide. The demands of his lower or animal nature must be held in obeyance to his superior intellectual endowment. His desire to accumulate property is a much higher aspiration than the desire to pamper and pet, and become the slave of his appetite, for it stands in the list of those qualities that belong to his higher nature.

Can we not argue then as it is man's nature to accumulate property, that he can therefore do so in that way that seems good to him? But the law and the common sense of all men, say no! If a man shall undertake to enhance the value of his property to the injury of his neighbor, the whole civilized world stands ready with a vote. Our law is supposed to have its foundation in justice when it refuses one man the privilege of taking something for nothing. Indeed this principle of justice underlies all the enactments of our law with reference to theft and fraud.

This may be fixed upon then as an axiom; a man has the natural and legal right to increase his property in any way that he pleases, provided, that he shall not interfere to the injury of the rights, person, or property of any one else. But if he may not accumulate property, regardless of the consequences to any one but himself, and his desire to do so is a higher law than that of mere appetite, it is senseless to argue that he may appease his appetite in any way he pleases without regard to the interests of other people.

The question then comes to this: can the eating and drinking of what one pleases interfere with the natural rights of others? If we answer in the affirmative then the boasted position of liquor dealers is gone.

If a man eats or drinks that which destroys his life, health, or his usefulness, he thereby injures, to some extent, every other man. But especially is his immediate community poorer in proportion to the amount of capital thus withdrawn from its resources. But when we come to reckon the evils of whiskey drinking, they are so numerous and of such fearful magnitude, that it is an absolute strain upon our charity to regard any man as both sane and honest who will contend for a minute that any man has any natural right to make a brute of himself in that way. It is now commonly known that to the account of intoxicating drinks, is charged nine-tenths of all the crimes brought into our courts. Can any man in his senses believe that it is the right of any man to drink that which will cause him to commit crime? Like all wrongs, these things come by degrees. The man first drinks occasionally with a friend, then by himself, then he neglects business to loaf around haunts of vice; his family is impoverished, he becomes reckless, and, under the influence of the "*narcotico acrid poison*," he commits murder or theft! Now it may be difficult to determine the exact time of his responsibility, but none will fail to charge up the crime, along with his neglect of family and business, to the drink that has at last brought him to ruin. Hence a man has no more right to drink that which will cause him to commit a crime than to commit the crime. itself. Again, it is certain that a man has neither the right to drink, nor the right to sell intoxicating beverages; for these are the acknowledged causes of nine-tenths of all the crime of the country to-day.

CHAPTER VIII.

PROHIBITION IS CONSTITUTIONAL.

Some years ago it was commonly said in opposition to prohibition that it was unconstitutional. In so grave an assembly as the Nebraska Legislature, only two years ago, it was regarded by a few men as unconstitutional. And though most people at the present time know better, yet it may not be wholly out of place, even in these articles, to give a few decisions on this subject. For the benefit of such as may have an interest in such things, I will quote from the fifth volume of Howard's Reports of the Supreme Court of the U. S.

Justice Carton said: "If the State has power of restraint by license to any extent, she may go to the length of prohibiting sales altogether." [Page 611.]

Hon. Justice Daniels said of imports when cleared of all duty and subject to the owner: "They are like all other property of the citizens, and should be equally the subjects of domestic regulation and taxation, whether owned by an importer or vender." [Page 614.]

And in reply to the argument that the importer purchases the right to sell when he pays duties to the government, the Judge says: "No such right as the one supposed is purchased by the importer. He has not purchased, and cannot purchase from the government, that which could not insure to him a sale independent of the law and policy of the States." [Page 617.]

Hon. Justice Grier says : " It is not necessary to array the appalling statistics of misery, pauperism, and crime, which have their origin in the use and abuse of ardent spirits. The policy power which is exclusively in the State is competent to the correction of these great evils, and all measures of restraint or prohibition necessary to effect that purpose are within the scope of that authority ; and if a loss of revenue should accrue to the United States from a diminished consumption of ardent spirits, she will be a gainer a thousand-fold in the health, wealth, and happiness of the people." [Page 632.].

Does some one say that the Hon. Justice was a little prejudiced in favor of the temperance cause ? I have only to answer that it does not appear in the decision. He has only said what his sound judgment and thorough acquaintance with law demanded of him. Hon. Justice Mc-Lean has also rendered several decisions.—

Among the many good things that he has said, I quote the following:

"A license to sell is a matter of policy and revenue within the power of the State." [Page 589.] "If the foreign article be injurious to the health and morals of the community, a State may prohibit the sale of it." [Page 565.] Again he says: "No one can claim a license to retail spirits as a matter of right." [Page 597.]

We could give almost any amount of this kind of authority, for supposing that Prohibition is constitutional. Indeed we know that it is, and will be, till the constitution shall be differently interpreted. One quotation from Chief Justice Taney, and we will desist from this constitutional investigation. He says: "If any State deems the retail and internal traffic in ardent spirits injurious to its citizens and calculated to produce idleness, vice, or debauchery, I see nothing in the constitution of the United States to prevent it from regulating or restraining the traffic, or from Prohibiting it altogether, if it thinks proper." [Page 577.]

So much for the constitutional right to prohibit the sale of intoxicating liquors. If any man asserts to the contrary, it is either because he is very ignorant, or very willful.

CHAPTER IX.

It is sometimes said that, although a prohibitory law may be perfectly constitutional, it is very inexpedient. For, say they, it cannot be enforced. *" We cannot enforce the law that we now have, and how could we operate a law of greater severity and strictness? It is not the penalties of law so much as the observance and respect of law that corrects public wrongs. And if we enact a law that is to become a dead letter, we simply educate the people to disregard the law, and insomuch as we influence the public mind, educate it to a disregard of our statutes."*
To me this is a special pleading that needs ventilation. It is based upon several false hypotheses. 1. This is false in the very nature of things which we will show in due time. 2. It takes for granted that all laws that deal with crime in general, are better regarded than a prohibitory liquor law would be. 3. That there is something in the traffic in whiskey that renders it impossible to be prevented. Of

course a special pleader may assume his premises and make a fair show in argument. But we intend to assail these premises, and show that they are not only not in existence, but the facts are quite averse to their declarations.

For the present I want to notice the utter impossibility of enforcing a license law. 1. To grant license to *honorable men*, and refuse it to all who are not "gentlemen of good moral character," is such a huge joke that one expects the whole plan to be tricky. Nor is the matter mended any by demanding that he shall file certain papers with the county or city clerk, containing the signatures of twelve freeholders in the precinct, asking that this "*gentleman*" shall have a license granted him to sell whiskey. For if there are that number of men who are mean enough to be the tool of the saloonist they can easily be made freeholders in any community where there is likely to be any trouble in obtaining a license. Hence these forms are the merest shams and only intended to blind the thoughtless with the appearance of justice. 2. The law forbids him then to sell to minors, one intoxicated, or one who is in the habit of becoming intoxicated, and then leaves him to decide who are such. Now I do not need to say that such a law is beyond the power of any common wealth to operate. It simply puts up

a blind before the public and then leaves these
rum-traffickers to sell to whom they please. 3.
The civil damage law sometimes tacked on to a
license law is so arranged that some injured
person must file the complaint. But before the
wife, or son, or daughter, or father, or mother,
would file such complaint, he would have to
lose self-respect, or be driven to desperation or
madness. And such persons would have so
little influence before the courts, that the cause
would be but little regarded. All opportunities
are granted to avoid and frustrate the ends of
the law. And the license system as a whole
has, in its history, been one of shame and scan-
dal to the people, and advantage to the workers
of iniquity. It is feeble and unjust in its nature,
and furnishes no means of enforcement.

Just now there are men to be found who
maintain that in those States where a prohibition law has been tried, the people have discov-
ered that it is powerless to restrain the vice of
intemperance, and therefore they are tired of it.
They claim that this is true because of the re-
cent elections. They tell us that the late
Democratic gains are owing to the fact that as a
party, there has been no disposition to meddle
with the temperance question; but that the
Republican party has unwisely permitted temperance men to dictate portions of its platform.

Now as much as I dislike to speak of politic-

al matters, yet necessity is laid upon me to
answer this logic of events. In all justice,
then, to all concerned, I must say that neither
of these parties, up to the present time, has
dared to take any definite action in favor of
temperance. And the little that the Republican party has dared to put into its state and
national platforms, on the subject of temperance, has been almost entirely against prohibition. That the last national platform contained
one of the most offensive planks on this subject,
that has ever been submitted to a civilized people, and that the thought of that article has
been adopted in substance by that party in
several of its State conventions, needs only to
be stated, for those who read know it to be a
fact. Not only so, but the little that it has said,
as in Maine and some other temperance States,
that is succeptible of another thought, is also
capable of a definition in every way suitable to
the whiskey traffic. These articles that have
had in them the slighest coloring of temperance
principles, have been framed with as much skill
as Grecian auricles ; framed so ingeniously that
they mean just what the reader or hearer wishes
them to mean. If, therefore, it is true that the
Republican party has lost by reason of any
position on this question, it is because its position has been on the wrong side of that subject,
that is, in opposition to prohibition. It is true,

however, that whiskey men are putting forth a
mighty effort to influence political parties, and
legislatures in favor of their traffic. And one
that knew no better, might be deceived into the
opinion that the money raised from one hundred
and sixty thousand saloons is furnishing an un-
answerable argument to both legislators and
judges, politicians, and parties. But it is not
true that there has been any decision by the
people, indicating their unwillingness to prohibit the sale of intoxicants,

This seems a proper place to notice the as-
sertion that is frequently made by men who
would gladly assist the rumseller, that there is
more liquor sold in and drunk under the Maine
liquor law than under the license laws. It is,
perhaps, true that those who assert this, are not
worthy of any attention, nor is it at all probable
that they will pay any attention to what we
may say on the subject, and yet we feel like
calling attention to a few facts, for the correctness of which our revenue Reports are respon-
sible. I will just call attention then to the
" *Revenue on Spirits in* 1873."

	Population.	Revenue.
Massachusetts under Prohibition	1,231,860	$1,674,460.07
Ohio under License	2,339,511	10,887.498.53
Illinois under License	1,711,951	3,727,790.43
Indiana under License	1,350,428	5,065,229.03
Maine under Prohibition	628,297	81,114.80
Maryland under License	687,049	1,084,396.40
New Hampshire under Prohibition	326,173	79,679.63
New Jersey under License	572,037	773,188.44

Now let it be remembered that the Prohibitory laws of Massachusetts and New Hampshire are a long ways from perfection, and then we will begin to see what the effect of such laws are. Let us balance two States, Maine and Maryland. Maryland had a few thousand the largest population and paid in revenue $1,084,386.40 under license, while Maine under Prohibition, with almost the same population, paid $81,113.80, or about one-thirteenth of the amount according to her numbers that was paid by Maryland.

Ordinary common sense ought to be sufficient to teach any man that a prohibitory law with any power of enforcement at all, would prevent, to a very great extent, the sale and use of intoxicating beverages. Rumsellers themselves know this ; and hence they use every possible means to prevent the enactment of such laws. And I am fully convinced that the facts will bear me out in this mild statement, that even imperfect as such laws have been, and as feebly as they have been enforced, they have reduced the sale and use of intoxicants, where they have been tried, seventy-five per cent below what has obtained in those States where the traffic has been licensed, and that crime in general has been abated in the same ratio.

Then let us be strong and quit ourselves like men. If we are to make war with the beast, the time has come for us to use at least ordinary discretion. If we will abate the nuisance, we must prohihit it. We must make our law to frcwn upon that traffic that is threatening our nation ; that is debauching and brutalizing and ruining our race. Not that we would discourage any attempt at the use of moral suasion. Much may be done in that way no doubt. But the evil can never be removed until we lay hold upon it with the hand of law, and thunder in the ears of those who are retailing this death and damnation to the poeple : "Take these thiings hence."

CHAPTER X.

A few semi-temperance men are yet prating about local option. Now after the severest exercise of charity, I am unable to look upon this as anything but a milk-sop, for rumsellers, while at the same time they would have credit with decent people for temperance principles. This law generally leaves it with the counties and cities of the first and second class to say, once in so often, whether the sale of intoxicating beverages shall be permitted in their respective localities or not. And if permitted, then rum may be sold without let or hindrance, or under such restrictions or limitations as may be found in the respective codes.

In favor of this, it is usually urged that a law can only be executed in those communities where the public sentiment has been cultivated up to the point of its enforcement, and therefore would be but a dead letter on the statute books where such education has not been had. And it is further argued that it is the best means of educating the people on the subject to cause them to have to vote on the subject once in two or three years. In answer to this, it must be said that law has always been in advance of the moral sentiment of those who violate it. And if we can only have such a law as will be in accordance with the wishes of all the people, we will never have a law of any kind. Nor would there be any particular need of any. Law is usually supposed to be beneficial in two respects. 1. In restraining the vicious. 2. In educating the ignorant. If a law should not be enacted till its principles shall first have come to be universally respected, then the purposes for which all laws are given are wholly thwarted. We would as well refuse the prescription of the physician till first we have recovered from disease. Is it said that they are not asking for universal respect, but only that general education that will make the enforcement possible? I ask, what do you mean by enforcement? Do you mean a perfect enforcement, in which no violation shall occur? I have statistics at hand, and they shall be forthcoming in due time, showing that the enforcement of a prohibitory liquor law is quite as possible, yea, even as probable, as that of any other law restraining vice. It is true that there have been many difficulties in the way, from the weakening enactments of legislatures, as nearly as possible, nullifying the law itself. Our laws are usually had by party legislation, the dominant party ruling. But these parties have been looking out for support, and hence, while they have courtesied to temperance influence, they have generally made obeisance to the rum power, enacting a law with one hand and killing it with the other. And yet with all the hindrances thrown in the way, its demands have been as well respected as any other law, in proportion to the enormity of the evil prohibited.

There is no philosophic reason why men may not be restrained from selling and drinking whiskey as well as prevented from any other crime against themselves or the community in which they live. Our law does not propose to license or permit infamy. It is based upon the presumption that, though the law may not be perfectly regarded, yet it can be, to some extent, at least, executed. And yet there are many reasons why a law prohibiting that nameless crime, can never be perfectly enforced, that do not exist as obstacles in the way of the enforcement of a prohibitory liquor law. The appetite for intoxicants is not natural, and the disposition to sell it, comes only from the love of money, without the necessary conscience to determine the right course by which the end shall be reached. And there can be found no reason, in the nature of things, why that crime may not be restrained as well as others.

But if the law by prohibiting the crime of

which we speak, could not be any better enforced than the law against adultery, still, it would
be a shame against our common humanity not
to prohibit it. It ought, at least, to free itself
from the charge of conniving at the crime.
The law can at least make it disreputable to
engage in the business.

But just what makes it necessary for us to
reach prohibition by local option no man can
tell. Why not approach the suppression of
every other crime in the same way as well as
that of intemperance? Suppose that our legislature in undertaking to prevent the lottery
stealing arrangements of the Sons of Belial
should give us local option on that subject?
And what would we think of the head and
heart of the man who would claim that such a
law cannot be executed in all communities, and,
therefore, should only exist in those places
where the people have been sufficiently educated on the subject? We might suppose that he
had some kind of interest in the business himself, or that he felt himself in need of the patronage of those who had! If a man should
argue that a law against murder will be violated
and disrepected in some localities and, therefore, that that crime should be dealt with by
license and local option, you would regard him
a fit subject for the next legislature! Now I
shall not say that local option is not better in

restraining the crime of stealing or murder or
that worst of crimes at the present time—rum-
selling, than no option at all, but I do say that
it is powerless to reach the cause and correct
the evil. It might stop a good many saloons in
country localities and in those counties where
they are not in much danger of being injured
by the trade, but in those cities and counties
where law is needed to prevent the vice, will be
the very places where local option will be powerless to administer the necessary correction.
Besides, if a county contains a city of the first
or second class that can muster a bare majority
for license, that city will sell about all of the
abominable stuff that the whole county otherwise would. The business of making drunkards and vagabonds will simply have been
taken out of the hands of the many and put
into the hands of the few.

But who knows just what is meant by local
option? Do we mean license in newly settled
territories till the temperance element will have
made war on the traffic in rum, or do we mean
Prohibition, till the whiskey element will have
raised the question and become the belligerents
in the campaign? The former is the usual
manner if not the only form in which it has as
yet made its appearance. This makes the tem-
perence men bear the expense, and labor against

established customs and prejudices. But in whatever form it may be presented I submit, that if the locality is less than a State which is to determine the privilege of selling poison, that local option is a failure, being wrong, essentially wrong, in its very nature, and perfectly impracticable, and barren of any very profitable results.

If I were a wholesale dealer in liquors and wished to monopolize the business, and were situated in a city of the first or second class and felt sure that license would carry in that place, then I would favor local option, since it would give me the trade that might otherwise be divided amongst a great many small dealers in rum.

If I were a politician of the first or second class—a mere politician, and felt that I must have office; that I could not live without office ; and that, in order to get it I must do something that would quiet the *"temperance fanatics,"* and yet not to any particular extent, injure the business of my whiskey friends, to whom I would have to look for the money to conduct the campaigns, then I might favor it; seeing that in that way I could "become all things to all men, that at least, by all means, I might gain some" votes. But why any man, with common sense, untrammeled with business or political aspirations should favor "local option " instead of prohibition is perfectly inexplicable.

CHAPTER XI.

WHAT HINDERS?

Our enemies are doing much to prevent the enactment and enforcement of wholesome laws in relation to the traffic in intoxicants. But our pretended friends are doing much more. This has always been true; it is the history of all reformations. The battle has to be fought by a few courageous men and women, who have to meet an organized and united enemy, and also to arrange for their own invalids, who never have any ability to resist the enemy. If they were only dead, they would be out of their own misery and our way. But no, they will neither live nor die for the good of the country. Whiskey men can give three millions to influence our general election. But if we were to ask a large class of so-called temperance men to make any reasonable expenditure of means for any such purpose, they would absolutely look at us a second time. Up to this time we have not made any effort that is worthy of the cause we plead.

Liquor men have been united and consistent; they have paid their money freely, and have evidently influenced legislators, judges, jurors, and officers of every grade and rank by their free distribution of mammon. True, we have provoked this liberality by endangering their craft. But we speak of facts, and not of moral qualities. To call these men liberal because they have given great sums of money for the purpose of having the privilege of continuing in their work of ruin, is to commit a serious blunder. But though there has not been one noble impulse in all they have done, yet we are not to be blinded to the fact that what they have done and are now doing have a potency to influence our law-making and law-executing powers in their favor. And though, for the good of mankind, the little that we have done for the cause of temperance, is many hundred times the amount ever performed by rumsellers, except for selfish ends, yet we are frank to confess that we have manifested but little of that good sense and liberal effort that the world had a right to expect of us. We have been wont to expect too much from the justness of our cause, without the proper means of bringing it before the people.

Again, our professional men have been unwilling to take any certain position on the subject. Editor, doctor, lawyer, and politician of every grade and rank, for fear of losing patronage, custom, or votes, either indirectly favor rumsellers or do so little as to be almost wholly worthless to the cause which they pretend to love. Many of these would be glad to work in the interests of the temperance cause if they were only sure that it would immediately triumph. Now the man who will rent a building for saloon purposes, who will sign a license bond, publish a whiskey advertisement in the columns of his paper, or manage a case in court for a saloon-keeper, vote for a license law, or for a party that supports it, in all or any of these ways assists the cause of the drunkard-maker, and, in so far, helps to ruin the country.

Even preachers have trimmed their sails before the popular breeze. They have feared that the church coffers would be empty, that their popularity would be endangered, and their audiences diminished, if their pulpits should give any certain sound in opposition to the death-dealing traffic. Many of them are entirely too religious for any such worldly considerations.

I do not speak of all preachers, nor all of any other class, for many of these are men of principle and common sense; have love for God and love for men, and are not too religious or too political to do their duty; but I speak of many in all these classes, who, by reason of

their selfish unwillingness to assume just re-
sponsibilities, are a standing disgrace and an
immense clog to the temperance reformation.

*The present political parties are a hinderance of
fearful proportions, to any effective legislation
against the whiskey business.* They occupy no
position on this question. A man may be just
as good a Republican or Democrat either, when
drunk as when sober. And, I am sorry to say
it, about as apt to have the support of the
leaders of these parties for any office that he
wishes, if he is in the habit of drinking as if
he were a sober man. Both of these bodies
are hopelessly divided on the question. Hence
neither can take any definite stand on the subject and live. It is impossible, therefore, that
either of these parties should give us any
effective legislation in the matter. Up to the
present time they have indicated their
worldly wisdom, in satisfying the temperance
element, by enacting a law that, on the surface,
shows a willingness to suppress the liquor traffic, but inwardly is wanting in every element
of vital energy. Thus they have aimed to
quiet all, giving to one class a law, and assuring the other that the law is impracticable and
therefore impotent to hinder their trade. This
is especially true with every license law that
has been enacted. And up to this time we can
hardly say that prohibition has been fairly tried

in a single State. Not that these legislatures are wanting the ability to frame a just and effective law, but they have had to save their parties.

Not only so, but the executive offices are filled by these same parties. And whatever may be the individual desires of the men elected, they are made to know that they are the representatives of a party whose policy is to have no position, and take no action, looking to the suppression of the liquor traffic. Of course we now and then get a man elected by one of these parties who will be true to his convictions, whether he pleases his political masters or not. But such a man is doomed to a short political career. The wire-workers of the party will not favor his second nomination. Most men, knowing these things to be so, and hoping for a continuation in office, will do as little as they can, for fear of offending one wing or the other of the party that elected them. Hence the condition of the political powers that now are, will, as it has been in the past, prevent both the enactment of righteous laws on the subject, and their enforcement when enacted.

Sometimes we are told that temperance men ought to attend the primaries and secure the nomination of good men, and in that way make themselves master of the situation. And yet men ought to know that no great good can be reached in this way. In the first place, the arrangements are made by the party manipulaters long before the unsuspecting temperance men have thought of it; for they work for pay, while we have no aim but the good of the country. And in most places, it is not difficult for saloon men to run in a few gravel trains and vote as many whiskey tickets at a primary election as they may want, to elect any man they wish to have attend the nominating convention. And, further, we have already found that, even though we should now and then succeed in securing the nomination and election of a good man in this way, yet the majority of them come to have respect to the recompense of reward; and the hope of continual support from the old party prevents the effort that ought to be made to prohibit the rum trade.

Again, it is said that we ought to ask our parties to adopt a prohibition plank in the platform, for this would certainly be definite enough to demand certain action of all its servants. This we have done. But our entreaties have been answered by repeated injuries. The leaders in these parties expect that temperance men, who earn an honest living, who are not seeking any office, and who have no monied interest in the question, except the general well-being of the country, can be lashed into the old party traces and made to support any

man at the polls, that "*the good old party*"
may nominate. But they know that it is not so
with whiskey men. They have a personal interest in the question, and will act with no
party beyond the precincts of individual advantage. Hence, they are assured of keeping us
without heeding our petitions, and also that they
would have to part company with the entire
whiskey vote, if the party should take any
definite position against the sale of intoxicating
beverages. The result is, that they have not
and will not take any position in the matter.

And if one of the parties should put a prohibitory plank in its platform it would commit
suicide in the operation. For it would lose its
entire whiskey vote, without gaining temperance votes enough from the other party to make
up the deficit. For, as much as we dislike to
own it, yet it is true, that many among us are
weak and sickly, and many sleep, and would
vote again with their old party, if not from
love for it, at least from hatred to the other
party against which they have contended so
many years. "Well, then, what do you propose
to do about it?" says the whiskey-loving politician of to-day. I answer for only one of the
friends of truth and justice, I propose to try to
unite all who love humanity, against this giant
evil against which we contend, not simply in per-
suading all we can to desist from the use of that

which can intoxicate, but in voting only for sober, honest, competent men. In doing this I have no doubt that a new political party will come into being that will dare to deal with the living issues of our age and nation. For, so far as I can now see, such a party is an absolute necessity, both to enact and to enforce a law prohibiting the manufacture, importation, sale, and use of that which can intoxicate. I have no doubt that if all the legal voters in the United States could be had to vote directly on this issue, License or Prohibition, that three out of every five would vote the latter. Hence I have hope for my country. It may indeed require time before men can be disentangled from their present political relations so as to act according to their better judgment in this matter, but the day will come. " *That which now lets will let till it be taken out of the way,*" but these powers that now oppose humanity; that now license the worst crime that has ever been committed, will be removed. I have ceased to expect the regeneration of either political party. But I hope and pray for their death.

A word to my friends and I am done. The success of our cause is the hope of our nation. Our people are becoming a nation of drunkards. And unless we can roll back these sulphurious clouds, we shall be as Sodom and Gomorrah, as Babylon, Nineveh. and Jerusalem. The floodgates of iniquity are opened wide, the crater is belching rivers of burning corruption. Up, and to your post. Be strong and quit you like men. The battle is to be fierce. God grant that it may be shortened for the elect's sake. Support no man, as you love your soul, for any office, who is unsound on the question of Prohibition. Work, work, and God bless the right.

www.ingramcontent.com/pod-product-compliance
Lightning Source LLC
Chambersburg PA
CBHW021225260626
47172CB00002B/606